TILLY'S PONY TAILS

Magic Spirit
the dream horse

PIPPA FUNNELL

Illustrated by Jennifer Miles

Orion
Children's Books

First published in Great Britain in 2009
by Orion Children's Books
a division of the Orion Publishing Group Ltd
Orion House
5 Upper St Martin's Lane
London WC2H 9EA
An Hachette UK Company

The Orion publishing group's policy is to use papers that are natural, renewable and recyclable products and made from wood grown in sustainable forests. The logging and manufacturing processes are expected to conform to the environmental regulations of the country of origin.

A catalogue record for this book is available from the British Library.

Printed and bound by CPI Group (UK) Ltd, Croydon, CR0 4YY

www.orionbooks.co.uk
www.tillysponytails.co.uk

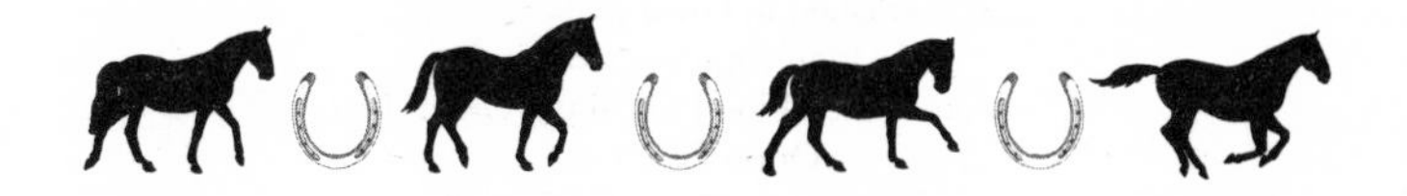

For my dear father,
George Nolan

For more about Tilly and Silver Shoe Farm –
including pony tips, quizzes and everything
you ever wanted to know about horses –
visit www.tillysponytails.co.uk

One

"When I was a girl, about your age," said Tilly's mum, as she ran the brush through her daughter's long dark hair, "I was mad, absolutely mad, about ice skating."

Tilly turned her head, curious to know more.

"Ice skating?"

She tried to picture it: her mum at an ice rink, gliding gracefully on a pair of blades. Doing turns and jumps.

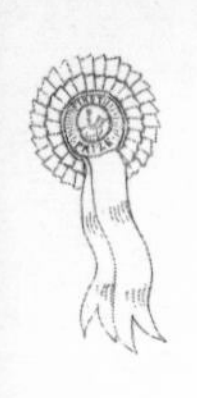

"Oh yes. I loved it," said Tilly's mum. "Almost as much as you love horses, Tilly."

To say that Tilly Redbrow loved horses was perhaps a bit of an understatement – desperately, wildly, crazy about them more like. You only had to take a peek in her bedroom to see that she was horse and pony mad. Every inch of wall space was covered in posters of the best breeds from around the world.

She spent as much time as she could exploring websites. Her favourites were www.girlshorseclub.com and www.ponybox.com. Here, she could read blogs and manage her own online equestrian team, losing herself in a world of horses that was all hers.

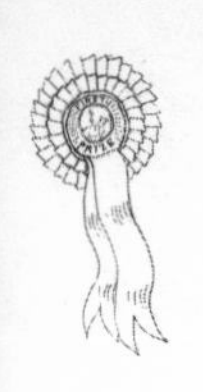

Scattered over the floor of her room were copies of her favourite magazine, *Pony*, which her dad bought for her once a month, from the big newsagent in the next village.

Tilly liked to gaze at the photographs of other *Pony* readers. These were girls who really did have their own ponies: Helen Davis from Somerset and her dappled grey Connemara, Prince, jumping a water ditch; Lucy Nicholson from Oxford clearing a round on her 13hh pony, Featherboy. Tilly wished it could be her in the photos.

At night, when she lay in bed, just before falling asleep, she would imagine galloping across the open prairie, or through the countryside, being carried away by her favourite fantasy horse: a mysterious black stallion called Magic Spirit.

"Tilly! *Tilly*!" said her mum, bringing her back to reality. "Do you want bunches or plaits?"

"Plaits."

"Always plaits," said her mum, as she started weaving sections of Tilly's dark hair, which was too long for Tilly to do herself. She refused to get it cut. It had been long ever since she could remember. It reached all the way down her back, and it was a pain to wash and look after, but she liked it.

"So did you have your own ice-skates then?" Tilly asked, when her mum had finished.

"Goodness, no. Far too expensive. Nanny Gwen and Grandpa Pete couldn't afford luxuries like that, so I had to make do with watching it on the telly. All those lovely fluttering outfits and sequins . . . so pretty.

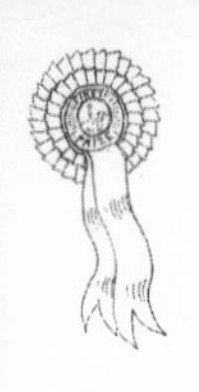

And I had lots of books and posters – just like you. I used to sit for hours looking at pictures of figure skaters and thinking to myself, why can't that be *me*? Oh well, too late now, I suppose. Silly ideas, eh?"

But in her heart, Tilly's mum knew they weren't just silly ideas.

She looked at Tilly's thoughtful reflection in the mirror, and knew how much her horse daydreams meant to her. She wondered how she could make these daydreams come true.

"How about some breakfast?" she said. "I've got some fresh bread from the bakers'. Maybe later we can make a cosy nest in the lounge, with blankets and cushions, and watch *The Horse Whisperer* again?"

"Okay," said Tilly. "But I'd better take Scruff for a walk first."

Scruff was the Redbrow family's dog, a long-haired Jack Russell, and he was

full of energy. The more exercise he got, the better. As soon as he heard the door opening he scampered towards Tilly, wagging his stubby tail.

Lower Norbury was a small place – a pub, a meeting hall and a post office, surrounded by a few stone cottages. Although it was much quieter than the nearby town of North Cosford, Tilly loved living there. She always enjoyed taking Scruff for walks down the main street on a sunny afternoon, smelling the flowers and listening to the birds.

Sometimes riders passed through, usually from Cavendish Hall, which was the exclusive boarding school and riding centre on the outskirts of North Cosford. Tilly had driven past it many times, stared up at its grand iron gates, longing to know what it was like inside. She'd heard that the pupils who went there were able to ride every day.

No one from *her* school, Heathwell High – where her dad taught – no one from there, as far as Tilly knew, was remotely interested in riding.

If only, she thought.

Suddenly three ponies emerged from the lane: two chestnuts and a bay. Their riders

were all girls, about Tilly's age, dressed in neat jodhpurs and designer t-shirts, with sleek blonde ponytails flowing from under their riding hats. They were definitely Cavendish Hall girls.

Tilly and Scruff stopped to admire the ponies. The bay, in particular, moved gracefully and his silky coat glistened in the sunlight. What a beautiful, magnificent creature, she thought. As the pony passed by, he stopped and leaned his nose towards her, gently sniffing at the bracelet around her wrist. The rider immediately apologised:

"Sorry. Don't worry – he's usually very good-natured. He won't hurt you or anything."

"I know," said Tilly, smiling. She reached out to the pony and stroked the white star on his forehead. He moved towards her, and started nuzzling her hand, as though her touch was blissful and soothing.

"What's got into you, Blaze?" said the rider impatiently. "He doesn't normally fuss over strangers. I *am* sorry."

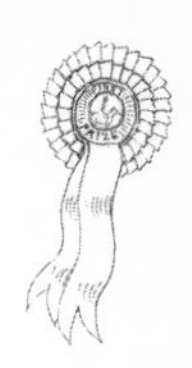

The other two ponies came up behind them, their riders whispering together.

"What's she doing?" whispered one of them, loud enough for Tilly to hear. "Come on. Let's go, or we'll be late for our dressage lesson."

With that, the group trotted on, leaving Tilly alone at the roadside. How lucky they are,

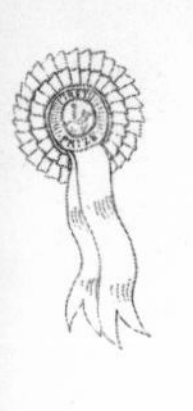

she thought, as she watched them disappear round the corner. And as she and Scruff ambled home, she kept asking herself, why can't that be me?

"So what's up, Tiger Lil'?" asked Mr Redbrow. He was the only person who called Tilly by her real name, Tiger Lily. He always knew when she was upset, because she would go very quiet and sit playing with her special bracelet.

"That old thing will break if you're not careful," he said, watching her twist it round and round her finger. It was strange looking,

made from woven horsehairs – black, plaited like Tilly's hair, and linked with a small silver clasp. Tilly had worn the bracelet all her life. She'd had it since birth, but no one knew where it came from – and there was little chance of finding out, because when she was very young, Tilly had been adopted.

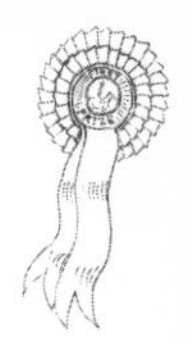

For as long as Tilly could remember, she'd been a Redbrow, and was happy to be so; but that didn't stop her from sometimes wondering who her mother and father were. And who *she* really was. The horsehair bracelet was her only link to the past, but it couldn't tell her anything.

Despite being happy with the Redbrow family, Tilly knew she was different. For a start, her thick, dark hair and olive skin made her stand out. Everyone in her adoptive family was fair and freckly, with tall, solid figures. Tilly was small and delicate. Her brother, Adam, who was born three years

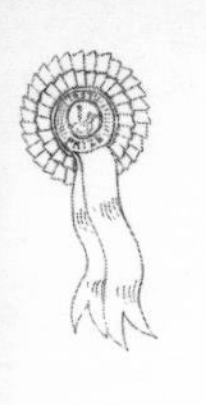

after the Redbrows had adopted Tilly, was taller than her already.

Tilly loved Adam, but he got on her nerves too. He was noisy and messy, and always hogged the computer. He would spend hours playing *Dungeons and Dragons* when Tilly wanted to chat online, or look up new pony websites. And he had an annoying habit of rushing to the computer table, just when he thought Tilly might do the same.

Tilly's dad sat down on the step and began tickling Scruff's ears.

"Did you see those three lovely ponies go through the village today?" he asked, hoping this would cheer her up.

Tilly just stared at her trainers and nodded.

"I was talking to Tom Cracknell from the post office earlier. He said that the girls who ride them are three of the best junior show jumpers in the county. They go to Cavendish

Hall and practise every day after school. There's been quite a lot of chatter about them in the local paper. Perhaps we should go along one day and watch them practise?"

"Everyone always goes on about the Cavendish Hall girls," said Tilly sulkily. "They're probably not *that* good."

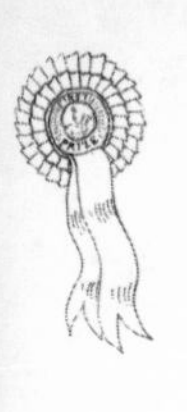

"Oh, come on, Tiger Lil', don't be like that – what have they got that you haven't, eh?"

Their own ponies, for a start, thought Tilly.

Two

The following day, Tilly and her mum were driving through the winding lane towards North Cosford. They were in a hurry to get to the supermarket on the edge of town, and then back in time to get dinner ready. But as soon as they turned onto the high street, their journey came to a halt. A line of cars was blocking the way.

"What is it?" complained Mrs Redbrow. "There's never usually traffic at this hour. Goodness, it's getting late."

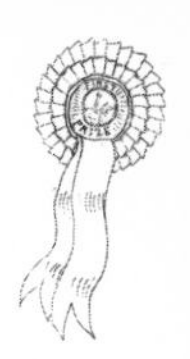

They sat for a while and Tilly stared out of the window, imagining how it would feel to escape from this standstill, to gallop away on Magic Spirit – no saddle, the wind all about her, completely free. She sighed to herself.

Suddenly they heard shouts from down the street. There was a lot of commotion, and people calling to each other.

"Perhaps we should turn back and go the long way round?"

"No wait. Something's happening," said Tilly. She leaned out of the window.

Ahead of them, a familiar shape was moving to and fro.

"What is it?" said her mum.

"It looks like a horse. It's trapped in the road, and everyone's crowding round and bothering it," said Tilly, concerned.

There were more shouts, and a mother and two children came running along the pavement. The horse started to rear and whinny, terrified, its eyes rolling alarmingly.

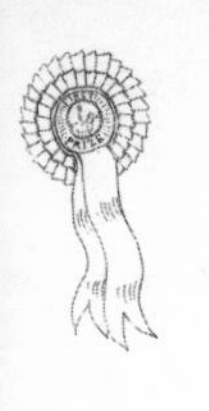

"I've got to help," cried Tilly, leaping out of the car.

"Tilly! Come back!" shouted Mrs Redbrow. "Get back here! Don't be silly – it could be dangerous!"

But it was too late. Her daughter was already halfway down the street, running in the opposite direction to everyone else.

The horse was thin. His mane was matted and his grey coat was covered in scratches and sores. He was clearly very distressed, dripping with sweat and shaking like a jelly. As soon as anyone tried to approach him, he would rear up on his hind legs with his ears flat back. But Tilly knew that he was acting out of fear rather than anger. He wasn't trying to hurt anyone. He was frightened.

A bald man in a blue suit tried to pull her away. He was shouting, telling everyone to get back – but Tilly understood that the

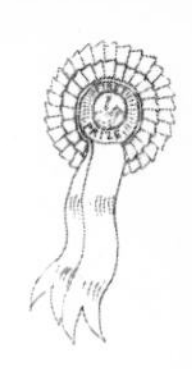

shouting was only making the distraught horse more upset.

"Someone call the police," the man yelled. "This crazy horse is going to kill someone if we don't get it under control!"

Tilly realised what she had to do. Suddenly everything around her seemed to fade and go quiet, as if the rest of the world had disappeared. All that remained was her and the horse.

She stepped quietly beside him, careful not to look directly into his eyes. And then she stood calmly, until he became aware of her. Somehow, her presence made him still.

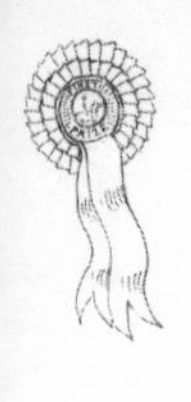

He stopped snorting, stopped swishing his tail and moved towards her.

"That's it, good boy," she said softly, as he lowered his head. "That's it, Magic Spirit. Don't worry. I'm Tilly. I'll help you. There boy, good boy."

With his head lowered, he allowed her to rub his nose. She felt his hot breath on her hands and saw the sadness in his eyes. He nibbled her sleeve and sniffed around her special bracelet, until slowly she was able to reach her hand up and take hold of his tatty

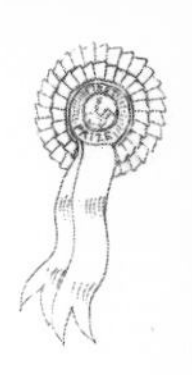

rope halter. Then, gently, she led him away, off the roadside and into the shelter of a nearby empty car park.

Twenty minutes later, after the crowds and traffic had cleared, a young woman arrived in a four-wheel drive towing a trailer. She got out, and after checking the horse for injuries, came straight over to Tilly.

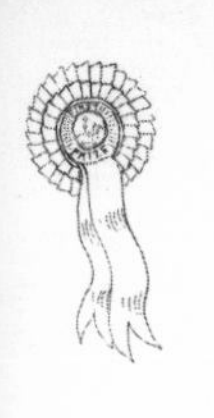

"You must be the girl who saved the day. I've heard what an amazing job you did."

"Are you from Cavendish Hall?" asked Tilly excitedly.

"Oh no. My father and I own a yard a few miles from here called Silver Shoe Farm. We're a busy livery yard with all sorts of horses, from ponies to competition horses. We have young ones, and even the odd rehab racehorse. You know, racehorses who need time and care to recover from their injuries."

The woman smiled. "I'm Angela, by the way."

I'm Tilly . . . short for Tiger Lily," said Tilly, knowing instantly that they were going to get on well.

"What will happen to the horse?" she asked. "His name's Magic Spirit . . . I think."

"Hmm, that's a good name. That's what we'll call him then. Well, no one seems to know where he came from. I assume someone must have abandoned him in one of the fields, and judging by his condition, I'm afraid it looks like he's had a pretty horrible

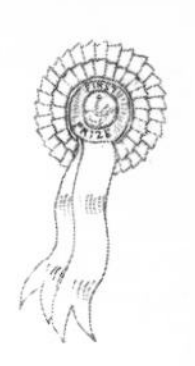

time. I'll take him back to Silver Shoe Farm and see what we can do. Part of what we do is help World Horse Welfare, who look after unwanted or cruelly treated horses. That's why I'm here to collect this poor boy. Thanks for your help, Tilly. It's quite incredible what you did, you know. Do you spend a lot of time with horses?"

Tilly looked at the ground. "Sort of," she muttered.

Angela looked surprised. "Well, you've obviously got a natural way with them."

"Tilly's pony mad," said her mum, coming to join them and standing proudly beside her. "She's got a room full of books and magazines."

"Well, that gives me an idea," said Angela brightly. "Tilly, you should come and spend a day with me, and I'll show you some of the horses at Silver Shoe."

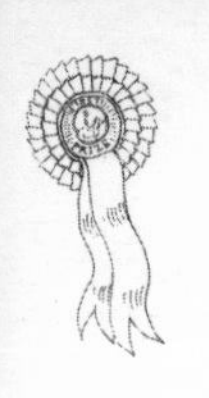

"*Really*?" gasped Tilly. "Can I?"

"Absolutely."

"And will I be able to help?"

"Of course," said Angela. "A special talent like yours shouldn't be wasted on books and magazines."

Three

All Tilly thought about for the rest for the week was her day at Silver Shoe Farm, which was arranged for Saturday. The time in between couldn't go fast enough. She sat through school, daydreaming about Magic Spirit and wondering if he was okay. Her Geography teacher had to repeat her name four times before he could get her attention.

And her best friend, Becky, said it was as if she was on another planet: Planet Pony.

When Saturday finally came, Tilly was awake at six in the morning. She lay in bed and checked through her latest copy of *Pony*, looking for ideas about grooming and handling – making sure a horse is tied

before grooming it; caring for its hooves. She wanted to impress Angela with her knowledge.

After a bowl of muesli and banana, Tilly's favourite breakfast, her dad drove her to the farm. At first they missed the turning, because the lane was half hidden by leafy, overhanging tree branches. It was like a secret hide-away.

When they finally found it, and saw the sign for Silver Shoe Farm, Tilly could feel butterflies in her stomach. They drove up an avenue of silver birches until they reached open fields for as far as the eye could see. In the middle of these fields was a group of cream buildings with reddish slate roofs, and

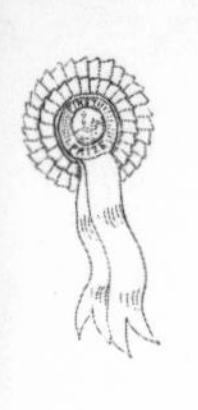

a couple of newly-creosoted black wooden barns.

"This must be it," said Mr Redbrow.

"It's perfect," whispered Tilly.

Angela met them in the yard, which was bustling with activity. There were three long stable blocks organised around a square patch of grass. Some of the horses were leaning their heads out, waiting for someone to give them some attention or, if they were lucky, the odd titbit. Others were being tacked up, or led through the yard, keen on the idea of having a few hours out in the paddocks.

A couple of girls, about Tilly's age, walked across the yard. One was struggling to carry a hay bale, and the other was holding a bucket of water.

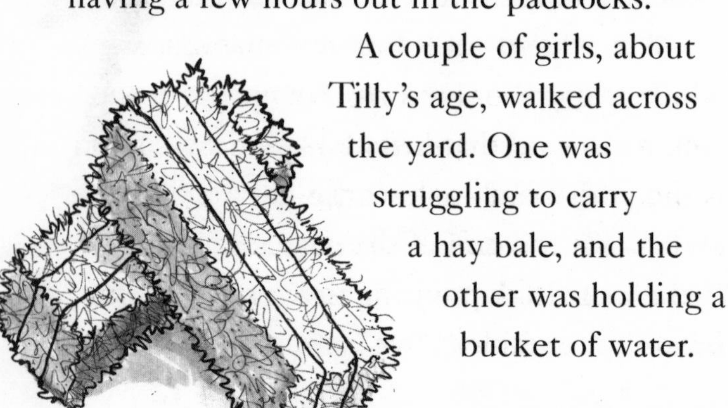

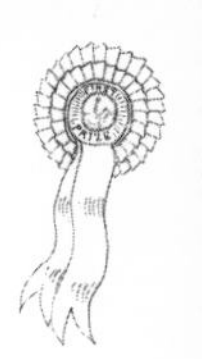

They looked at her and smiled.

"That's Cally and Mia," said Angela. "They're here every weekend. We're a friendly bunch. You'll definitely be made to feel welcome at Silver Shoe. I've told everyone about you. Let me show you around, and then I'll introduce you to some of our horses and people."

Tilly said goodbye to her dad, and didn't feel at all nervous about being left without him. She and Angela walked the length of the yard, and Angela explained that they had twenty stables and thirty acres for grazing.

"We've also got lots of woodland nearby, which is great for hacking. Behind us is the tack room, and that little building next to it is the club room – where the gang like to chill out at the end of the day. And over there," she said, pointing to a large building beyond the stables, "we have an indoor

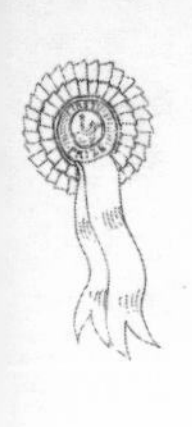

menage for the winter months, and a big outdoor training area, with a gallop for the racehorses and eventers – that's where all the best stuff happens."

"Like what?" asked Tilly.

"Why don't you come and see for yourself?"

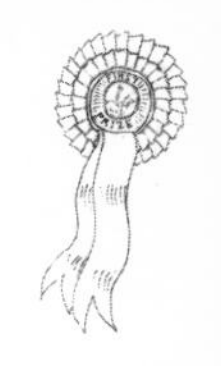

The outdoor arena was a huge grass area, lined with trees, with a sand school and a smaller pen for lunging, surrounded by wooden fencing.

"There's Red Admiral," said Angela. "He's a young thoroughbred. He's been injured recently; it's going to be a long time before he sees a racecourse."

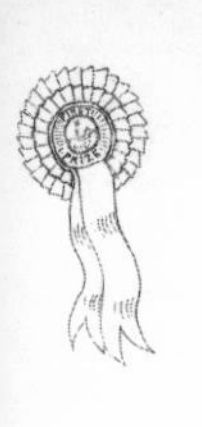

They stopped at the fence and watched the proud chestnut-red horse being led round the pen. Eventually his handler, an old man in a checked shirt, brought him over to say hello.

"So, you must be Tilly," he said. "Very pleased to meet you. I'm Jack Fisher, Angela's father. I'm the owner of Silver Shoe – if you need anything, just come and ask. Angela's told me all about your efforts with that rescue horse the other day. Quite impressive."

"You mean Magic Spirit?" said Tilly, glancing between him and Angela. "Where is he? Can I see him? Is he doing okay?"

"He's . . . um . . . he's having a bit of a hard time, Tilly," said Angela slowly. The tone of her voice was worrying.

"He's a tricky character all right," added Jack Fisher. "But it's not unusual for rescue horses to be difficult, especially if they've been treated badly. We've had to keep him in a separate barn – he's kicked all the walls and chewed the wood. He hates the other horses and he won't take human contact.

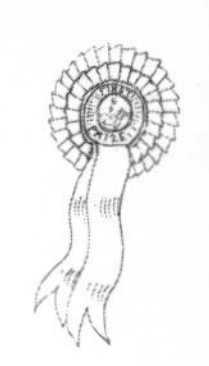

Every time someone has tried to get near, he's reared. It's been almost a week and I desperately want to get him wormed and vaccinated, but at the moment he's too dangerous."

"I could help," said Tilly. "I think he trusts me – I could reassure him."

"Oh, I don't know about that," said Jack, swatting a fly away. "We promised your dad we'd look after you – we can't just send you into a barn with a traumatised animal. That's a crazy idea."

Tilly was frustrated.

"There's something about this girl though, Dad," Angela urged quietly. "Honestly, she's got a special way from what I've heard. I reckon we should at least try – for Magic Spirit's sake. Don't worry, I'll make sure she's safe and we won't take any chances."

"You'll drive me to an early grave one of these days," muttered Jack, rubbing his head. Red Admiral started to snort impatiently. "Look, I've got to get back to work with him. You girls go over to the barn

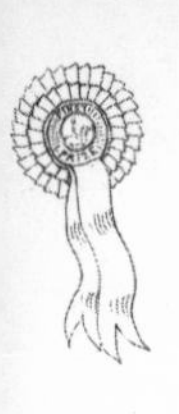

and do what you can for Magic Spirit, but any sign of trouble and you're straight out of there, right?"

"Right," they both said together, smiling.

Four

Magic Spirit was in a small black wooden barn at the end of the yard.

"Well, he's quiet at least," said Angela. "In the night he was whinnying and banging constantly. We could hear him from the house."

She and Tilly peered inside. The stall was dark, and at first Tilly couldn't see anything, then she saw the flash of his eyes. He was looking at her from the shadowy corner.

"Hello, Magic," she murmured. "It's me

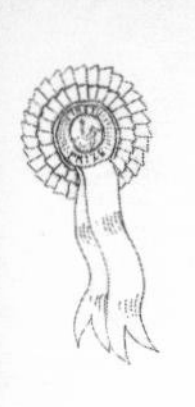

again. It's Tilly. Don't be frightened."

Magic snorted and shuffled through the wood-chip bed that had been laid down for him, then he stepped forward inquisitively.

"Can I go in?" asked Tilly, looking at Angela.

"In a minute. See how he is first. Remember what my dad said – no one's been able to get near him yet, so we mustn't take any risks. It looks like he's eaten some of his hay at least."

Tilly leaned over the door of the barn and reached out her hand, so that Magic, when he was ready, could come and greet her. A minute passed, and then slowly he came closer.

"Hello there," said Tilly in a soft voice, as she stroked his nose. Magic started sniffing at her bracelet, as he'd done the first time they'd met each other.

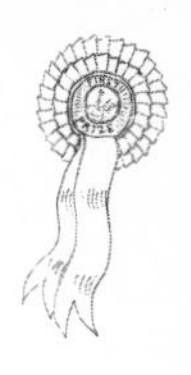

"That's amazing," whispered Angela, watching from behind. "Amazing."

After a while, Tilly unbolted the bottom half of the stable door.

"I don't think you should do that," cautioned Angela. But in her typical determined way, Tilly had already made up her mind. She pulled the wooden door just wide enough for her to slip inside. Then she waited. She didn't go in immediately, because she knew that Magic would let her know exactly when he was ready for her to enter his space. He stepped backwards and rubbed his head against the stable wall. Tilly could see the splinters in the wood panels where he'd tried to kick through.

Eventually, she crept into the entrance and stood beside him. He allowed her to stroke his neck and shoulder. She was careful not to touch any sore patches, or make any sudden movements that would frighten him. This was something she knew about from reading lots of pony care books, but she had a different kind of knowledge as well. There was a special connection between them – something that

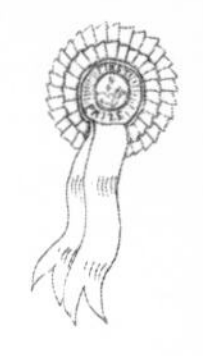

couldn't be learned from any book.

Outside, by the door, Angela was watching, her mouth open.

"Maybe I should call the vet right away," she said to herself. "Maybe Tilly can keep him calm while he gets checked over."

She reached into her pocket for her mobile phone.

Moments later, Jack Fisher entered the yard, leading Red Admiral, the haughty young thoroughbred. They had finished their training for the morning.

"Quick," Angela called over to Jack, in a loud whisper. "Come and look at this."

Jack crossed the yard, with Red at his side. They stopped a few feet from the stable and glanced in.

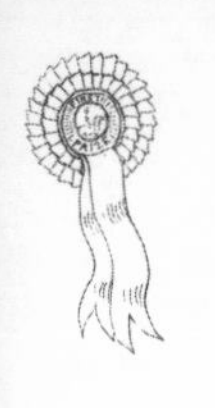

"Well I'll be blown," said Jack. "In all my years of . . . I don't quite believe it . . . you said the girl had a special knack but *this* is extraordinary!"

Unaware of their audience, Tilly and Magic carried on getting to know one another. Tilly could see that despite his scruffy appearance and bony body, Magic was a tall, athletic-looking horse. In an instant, she imagined that he'd make a great show jumper; she saw herself riding him at Olympia, skilfully clearing the biggest fences. Magic Spirit nodded, as if he was reading her thoughts and agreeing.

Suddenly, a gust of wind blew an empty shavings bag across the yard, startling Red. He spooked and shot forward, snorting. Magic instantly leaped towards the door, his ears flat back, baring his teeth.

Shocked, Tilly stumbled away from him, nearly falling flat on her back. She picked herself up and got out of the way as quickly as she could. Her heart was beating faster than ever. Angela took hold of her arm and pulled her to safety, then shut the barn door.

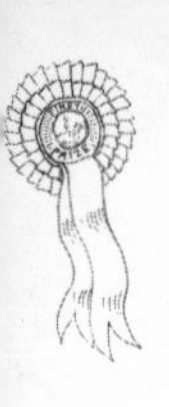

Meanwhile, Jack was busy trying to settle Red Admiral.

"Goodness me," said Angela, brushing straw from Tilly's jacket. "Are you okay? You're not hurt are you? I'm so sorry . . . we should never have let you—"

Tilly took a deep breath.

"I'm all right. Honestly. It wasn't his fault. He was frightened."

But Tilly was shaking all over. Her hands were trembling, and no matter how much she tried to relax, she couldn't stop them.

"Oh dear," said Angela, frowning. "Let's go and have a nice hot drink. I think we need one."

Five

The clubroom was warm and cosy with scruffy, comfy sofas and a little kitchen area. Across the walls were photos of riders and their horses, either jumping, racing or holding trophies. Tilly noticed one of Angela, standing proudly beside a winning horse. On the far side of the room, there was a notice-board, which had rosettes pinned to it and

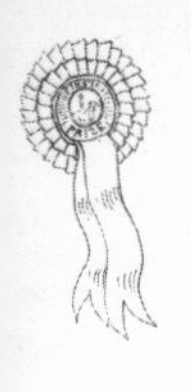

several notes advertising second-hand riding gear, hay for sale, and paddocks to let.

Tilly looked around while Angela made them hot chocolate. She added marshmallows and carried them over to the sofa.

"There you go," she said, passing Tilly a mug. It was chipped, but Tilly didn't mind.

"At Cavendish Hall they have designer mugs, you know," said Angela, watching Tilly cradle the chipped mug. "They get them specially made and printed with their school crest. And their club room is

really smart – it's got a surround sound TV and a DVD player and power showers."

"I like it here," said Tilly.

"Good," said Angela, relieved. "I'm glad – and I'm also glad," she added, raising her eyebrows and scraping back her long, red hair, "that you weren't hurt by Magic Spirit. No matter how well you get on with the ponies here, Tilly, you've got to remember that they can be unpredictable sometimes. I'll get the girls to go through the rules of safe handling with you, and then maybe you can help with some of the grooming and mucking out. How would that be?"

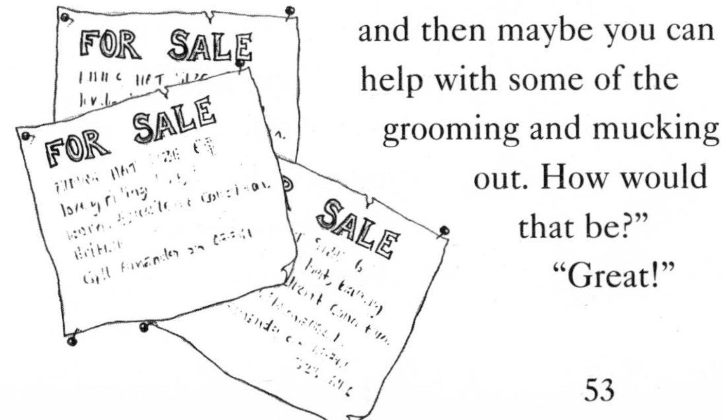

"Great!"

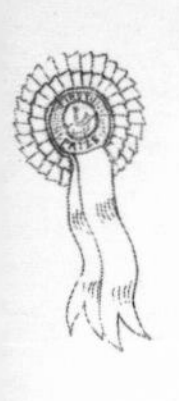

Just then, the two girls Tilly had seen in the yard earlier walked in. Both of them were busy texting on their mobiles, then they went straight to the kitchen to make themselves a drink.

"Cally. Mia. Come over and meet Tilly. She's visiting for the day."

They both turned and smiled.

"Hiya," they said together.

"Hi," said Tilly shyly.

"Hey, I recognise you," said Cally. "You go to Heathwell High, don't you? We're in the year above you – Miss Bright's form. Do you want a biscuit?"

She offered Tilly a packet of biscuits.

"Thanks," said Tilly.

"So have you got a pony, then?" asked Mia, sitting down beside them. She was small, with pale skin and short blonde hair. Cally was taller, and had lots of black curls and train-track braces on her teeth.

"No," said Tilly. "Have you?"

"Well, sort of. Me and Cally share one – we've been best friends for ever, and our

mums decided it would be more affordable that way. We share all the expenses—"

"And all the work," added Cally.

"And then we both get to ride her – not at the same time of course!"

"You're so lucky," said Tilly.

"You'll have to come and meet her. She's lovely – her name's Rosie. Would that be okay, Angela? Can we take Tilly to see Rosie? We're about to groom her."

"Why not?" said Angela. "Don't forget the safety rules though, girls."

Tilly finished her hot chocolate and followed the girls back to the yard.

"First things first," said Mia sensibly, leading Tilly to the tack room. "If you're working close to a horse or pony, always wear sturdy boots.

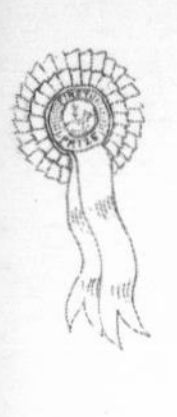

Your trainers won't give you any protection if they tread on your feet!"

Tilly looked at her trainers.

"I've only got these," she said.

"Don't worry. I've got a spare pair you can borrow."

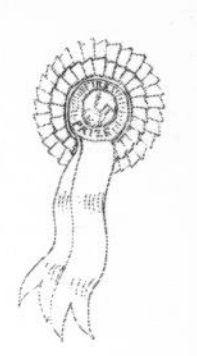

She handed Tilly a pair of brown jodhpur boots. Tilly pulled them on. They were the right size.

"Have them if you like," shrugged Mia. "They don't fit me anymore."

"Wow! Thanks."

They walked over to Rosie's stall, and Tilly loved the feeling of wearing the boots – they made her feel like a proper horsewoman. Cally opened the stable door and started making clucking noises. Rosie leaned her head out and began to nuzzle Cally's neck. She looked very friendly – a strawberry roan – but Tilly couldn't help feeling a little bit anxious after what had happened with Magic Spirit.

Mia carried a grooming kit over.

"She loves being groomed," she said. "We do it as often as we can because it keeps her coat nice and healthy – and it makes her look beautiful. But most of all, she likes the attention! She's such a princess!"

Rosie lowered her head.

Cally checked the headcollar.

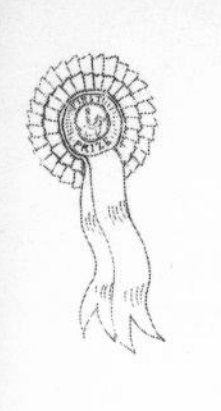

"Is she safely tied?" asked Tilly, remembering what she'd read about in *Pony* magazine that morning.

"Yep. Safe and sound," replied Cally.

"But we always use a quick-release knot," added Mia. "So that she can pull free if she gets scared. Some horses don't like the feeling of being constrained and it makes them panic."

She reached into the grooming kit box and pulled out a brush. Tilly recognised it as a Dandy brush: a stiff-bristled brush used to loosen dirt. Mia started rubbing the Dandy in circular motions across Rosie's body, being very gentle around her thinner-skinned and bony areas. She talked to Rosie the whole time, whispering nice things and telling her how beautiful she was.

"We start at the top of the neck and then work our way down to her rear, and then switch sides – if she was covered in thick mud we'd use a plastic curry comb," explained Cally.

HOOF
TAIL &
MANE
detangler

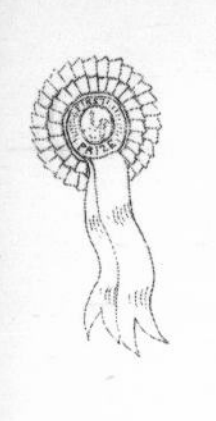

"Once all the dirt is loose, we comb her mane and tail, and then we use the softer bristled brush to get rid of the dirt. We scrape that brush with a metal curry comb to get the grease and dust out."

Once Cally had done all of this, she picked up an old tea towel.

"This is a stable rubber – it removes any remaining scurf and smoothes her coat. It makes her coat look super shiny. Then we'll use a comb for her mane and tail, and conditioning spray, which makes the comb glide through her tail. Do you want a go?"

Tilly took the brush in her hand and allowed it to glide across Rosie's body. As she did this, a beautiful sheen appeared on the pony's coat. Then Cally took the body brush and showed Tilly how to groom Rosie's face, making sure not to bother her eyes or the sensitive

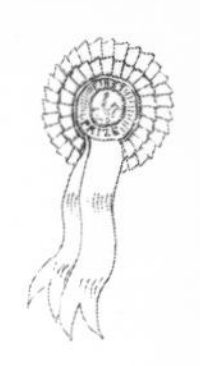

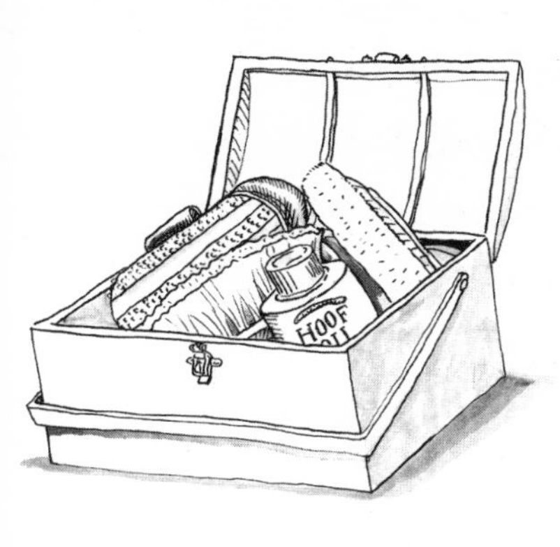

bits around her nose and ears.

"And finally," said Mia. "We check her legs and clean her hooves."

Carefully, she ran her hands down Rosie's legs, feeling for any cuts or swellings. "It's important because if you get straight on and ride without checking, you could cause more damage, or even lameness.

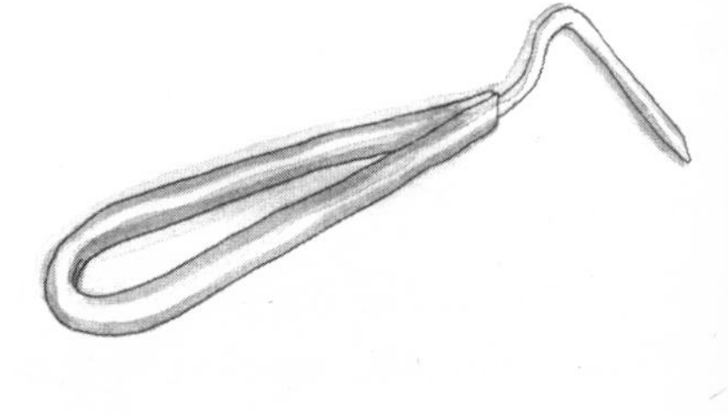

"One of Angela's rules is that we always pick the horses' feet out with a hoof pick before coming out of the stable – it keeps the yard tidier and Angela likes that. If the horses are turned out it's the first thing we do when we bring them in."

Just then Angela popped her head over the stable door. "How are you getting on?" she asked. "Have you remembered to paint her hooves with the special hoof oil? Tilly,

did the girls tell you we keep a notebook in the tackroom listing all the dates of when our horses were last shod – normally a set of shoes lasts for five to six weeks."

Tilly watched, trying to take in all this new information and eager to have a go herself. One day Magic Spirit might let me groom *him*, she thought.

Before Tilly left Silver Shoe Farm that day, she made sure she paid one last visit to Magic Spirit. At first she was nervous, because of what had happened earlier, but she knew that if she let her worry get the better of her, it would make Magic Spirit nervous too. She leaned over the bottom half of the stable door and reached her hand in. To her relief, he was calm and gentle with her. He came over and let her stroke his neck, and gradually she started to scratch harder. He nuzzled the back of her neck.

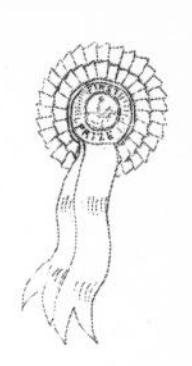

"You scratch my back and I'll scratch yours," Tilly giggled, as Magic tickled her, sending goosebumps down her spine.

"Good boy," she said quietly. "Don't worry, I'll be back soon – I hope."

Then her mobile buzzed. It was her dad, texting to let her know that he was waiting in the lane for her. Time to go home.

Angela was in the yard, helping Cally and Mia to saddle up Rosie.

"Well, I hope you enjoyed yourself, Tilly," she said.

Tilly had had a great time, but when she looked at Rosie she also wished she'd had a chance to do some actual riding. Sensing this, Angela smiled.

"You'll have to come back soon, and maybe we'll get you up on one of the ponies . . ."

Tilly grinned.

"And you're welcome to help us groom Rosie again," said Cally.

Rosie fluttered her eyelashes.

"Cool."

"We'll see you on Monday," said Mia.

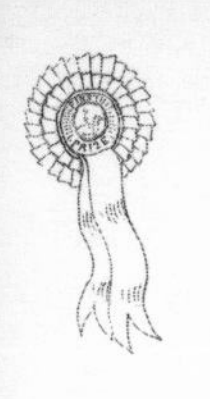

For a moment Tilly was puzzled, then she remembered that they went to the same school.

"Yes. See you then," said Tilly, as she opened the five-bar wooden gate, and climbed into the passenger seat of Mr Redbrow's car. He'd been sitting doing the crossword while he waited for her to say her goodbyes. Adam was in the back, eyes fixed on his Gameboy.

"Well?" said Mr Redbrow. "How was it then?"

"Aaah!" sighed Tilly, sinking into her seat and smiling. "Where do I start?"

Six

Tilly talked and thought about nothing but Silver Shoe Farm for the next few days. At supper on Saturday, it was the latest colours for jodhpurs. At breakfast on Sunday, it was hoof picks and body brushes. At lunchtime, it was how to catch a difficult horse. And in the evening, it was back to jodhpurs. Tilly was in her element. Her mum and dad were pleased, but by the fourth time they'd heard her detailed descriptions of Magic Spirit, Red Admiral and Rosie, they were somewhat worn out.

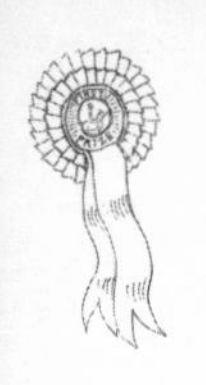

"You know," said Mrs Redbrow, when Tilly had gone to bed. "She's so crazy about ponies – it would be great if we could organise some riding lessons for her. She'd be thrilled."

"I'd better go for that promotion then," said Tilly's dad, smiling.

On Monday morning, Tilly's best friend, Becky, called for her. They walked to the bus stop, to catch the 275 to school. On the journey, as usual, they listened to music on Becky's iPod, sharing the headphones as they sang along.

"Did you watch *The X Factor* on Saturday? Who did you think was best?" asked Becky.

"I didn't watch any television this weekend. I was busy. I was at Silver Shoe Farm – *all* day," said Tilly.

"Ooh. Big deal," said Becky, pulling a face and adjusting her headphone.

Becky had been Tilly's best friend ever since primary school. She didn't share Tilly's mad passion for ponies – she thought it was crazy, and liked to wind Tilly up. Tilly, in turn, liked to wind Becky up about her obsession with winning *The X Factor* and joining a girl band. But even though the girls had different interests they always had fun together and that's what mattered most of all.

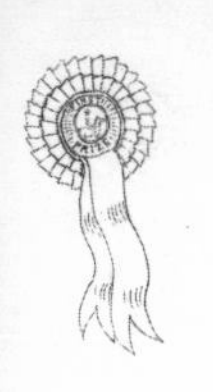

The last lesson of the day was History. Tilly stared out of the window and wondered how she could help Angela and Magic Spirit. She remembered that she had the latest copy of *Pony* in her bag. When no one was looking, she pulled it out and slipped it in front of her textbook, so that she could read it while pretending to do her work.

She turned straight to the problem page, where readers had written in asking for advice, and soon she was lost in ideas about saddlery and training tips. She studied a letter from a girl who kept falling off her pony whenever he bucked. She wanted to know how to stay on. Tilly tried to imagine what she would do in that situation – get my legs forward, sit back, and stick like glue, she thought, just like cowboys at Rodeos. And to her surprise and pleasure, that's what the reply to the letter suggested too!

Moments later, Tilly felt a sharp jab in her ribs. It was Becky, warning her that Mr Baxter, the History teacher, was coming over.

He wasn't impressed.

"Tilly Redbrow! That doesn't look like the Norman Conquest to me! Hand it over, please!"

Tilly gave her teacher the magazine. She could feel everyone in the class looking at her. Mr Baxter leafed through it, turned his nose up, and then marched over to his desk and placed it in one of the drawers. Two boys in the back row started whispering Tilly's name and making stupid neighing noises.

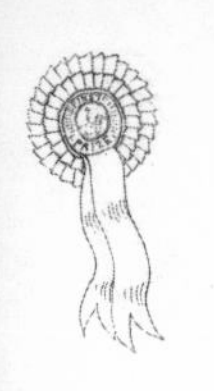

"Ignore them," whispered Becky.

After the bell, Tilly waited at Mr Baxter's desk and asked for her magazine.

"I'll give it back to you, Tilly, but I'm not best pleased. How will you pass your exams if you don't pay attention in class? As a punishment, I want you to write five hundred words on the history of equestrianism. Got that? Five hundred words. Equestrianism. On my desk by tomorrow morning."

"Absolutely!" said Tilly, smiling. That's not a punishment, she thought.

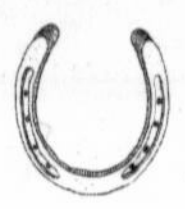

Tilly and Becky caught the bus home. Sometimes they got a lift with Tilly's dad, but he often had to stay late for meetings. The girls walked through the village, picking leaves from the trees as they went and talking about Mr Baxter's funny hair. Becky was convinced he wore a wig. Tilly thought it was a hair transplant.

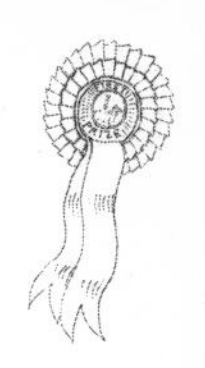

"Do you want to come round to mine?" asked Becky. "We could do our homework together, then go on the Nintendo DS. My brother's got a new game. He'll let us borrow it if he's in a good mood."

"I can't tonight," said Tilly. "I promised Baxter I'd write that horse essay."

"You're not *really* going to do that are you? He won't remember by the morning!"

"But I want to," said Tilly.

"Suit yourself."

They said goodbye and went their separate ways.

When Tilly got home, she made herself a hot chocolate and went straight to the computer. She printed some information from a website called www.horsesmart.co.uk, and then sat at the kitchen table and worked on her essay until it was dark, using her best handwriting and decorating the margins with drawings of ponies.

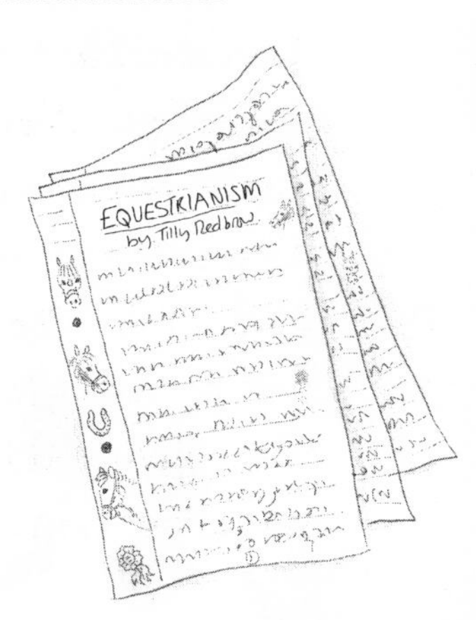

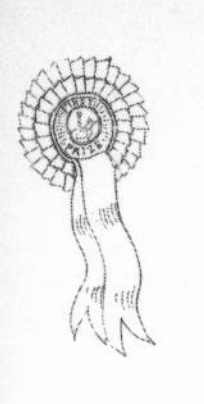

The horse research took up so much space that Mr Redbrow had to take his marking into the living room when he got home, and Mrs Redbrow was forced to prepare the supper on the tiniest square of tabletop. She kept smiling to herself though, because she'd never seen Tilly take so much care over homework before.

The following morning, Tilly took her essay straight to Mr Baxter. As Becky had predicted, he seemed confused when she handed it to him.

"Five hundred words on the history of equestrianism," said Tilly, out of breath because she'd run all the way to his classroom. "Except – I hope you don't mind – but it's not five hundred words, it's more like a thousand."

Mr Baxter just scratched his head and nodded.

Seven

Next day at school, Tilly went to find Becky in the lunch queue, so they could sit together as always. As she made her way between the canteen tables, she heard her name being called. The voice was familiar. She turned and looked.

"Tilly! Tilly! Over here!"

It was Cally. Mia was with her. They were both sitting at the long table, eating jacket potatoes. Tilly walked over.

"Come and sit with us," they said, smiling.

“Oh . . . I don’t know if I can,” said Tilly anxiously, looking back at the queue where Becky was waiting for her. She really wanted to sit with Cally and Mia, but she didn’t want Becky to feel left out. In the end she hovered at the end of the table, twiddling one of her plaits.

“Guess what?” said Mia excitedly.

"Thanks to you, Angela was able to get the vet to look at that new rescue horse."

"You mean Magic Spirit?" said Tilly, wide-eyed.

"Yeah, after you visited him on Saturday, he was really calm – the calmest he's been since he arrived at the stables. He obviously trusts you. The vet checked him over and says he'll be okay."

"He's been vaccinated and wormed, and treated for his sores, and now he needs lots of feeding up," added Cally. "But with a bit of love and care we'll get him right. Angela never turns a horse away. Even though she loves training thoroughbreds, she'll help any animal. Hey, when are you coming to the farm again? Don't you miss Magic Spirit?"

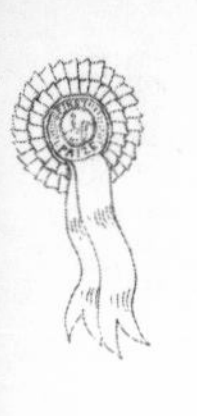

"Come with us after school," said Mia. "My mum picks us up and drops us off at the stables every evening. She won't mind giving you a lift too."

Tilly felt overwhelmed. She couldn't stop smiling.

"If that's okay . . . that would be great, thanks."

"Cool. We'll meet you at the front gates, four o'clock. See you then."

Tilly walked away and went to find Becky, who had already got her lunch and was sitting at their favourite table, beneath the big window. She was prodding a lump of green jelly with the end of her spoon, and staring into space.

"There you are," she said, as Tilly joined her. "I thought you'd abandoned me."

And although Becky said it jokingly, there was something in the way she said it that made Tilly feel guilty.

At five to four, Tilly met her dad as he was walking from the Maths block.

"Can I go to Silver Shoe with Cally and

Mia?" she said breathlessly. "Mia's mum can give me a lift—"

"I suppose so," said her dad, almost dropping a pile of textbooks. "Make sure you're back in time for tea."

Tilly ran all the way to the front entrance. She felt relieved that Becky had already disappeared to the music department for her weekly singing lesson.

Cally and Mia were standing at the gates, busily texting on their mobiles, as usual. They greeted Tilly and then the three of them climbed into a huge midnight blue four-wheel drive.

Mia's mum was driving. She was young looking and very glamorous, with a stylish bob and long fingernails. Not like a mum at all, thought Tilly – more like a big sister.

"How was work?" said Mia, then she looked at Tilly and explained. "My mum owns a hair salon in North Cosford. It's called Dream Cuts. Do you know it?"

"No. My mum cuts my hair," said Tilly, embarrassed.

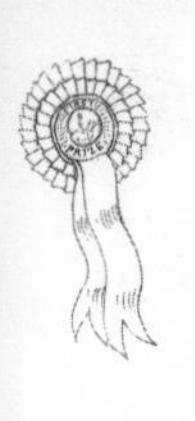

"Well, you've got lovely hair," said Mia's mum. "I can tell it's really thick and healthy. I reckon it would look nice with some layers – make you look a bit older."

Tilly blushed. Meanwhile, Cally and Mia started rummaging through a sports bag, pulling out jeans and t-shirts and changing into them.

"We're not allowed to go to the stables in our uniform," moaned Cally. "In case we get mucky. Here, you can borrow this," she said, handing Tilly a pale pink polo shirt.

They arrived at Silver Shoe Farm and Tilly felt the same rush of excitement she'd had the first time she saw it, appearing out of the fields, through the tunnel of trees. It was

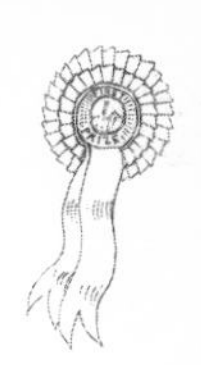

a lovely evening – late April, and the trees were fresh with blossom and leaves.

The stable yard was busy. Two small ponies were having their manes pulled. And on the other side of the yard, there were some bigger horses being tacked up. The horses seemed to like each other's company and the atmosphere was very friendly. Tilly spotted Angela straightaway. Her wild red hair made her stand out. As soon as she noticed the three girls she came over.

"Hello, you lot. How nice to see you again, Tilly. Magic Spirit will be pleased. I suppose the girls have told you the good news about the vet. We're delighted with the progress Magic's making. He's definitely eating well. Doesn't seem to want to come out of his barn though. Oh well, we'll give it time."

She looked at Mia and Cally.

"Rosie's in the paddock. She was turned out after you groomed her this morning. She's had a nice day grazing with some of the other ponies. If you go and find Duncan, he'll help you catch her. Which of you is riding today?"

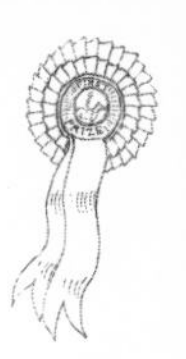

"*Me*!" they both said together, exchanging looks.

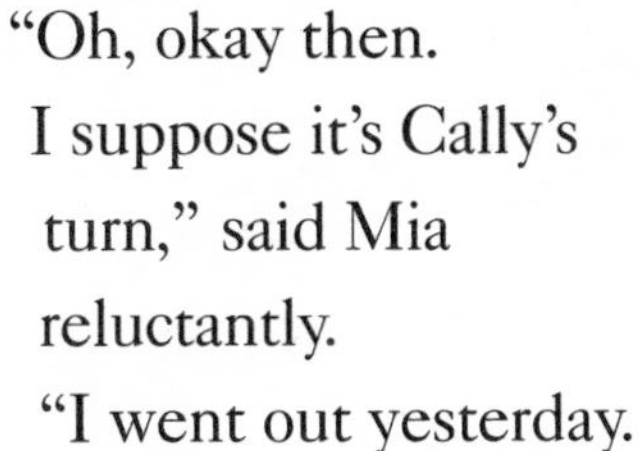

"Oh, okay then. I suppose it's Cally's turn," said Mia reluctantly. "I went out yesterday. Come on, Tilly, let's go and see Magic Spirit."

She linked her arm through Tilly's and swept her across the yard, towards the small barn, while Cally went to the tack room to get ready for her ride.

"Who's Duncan?" asked Tilly.

"He's Angela's head boy. He helps her run the stables. He's a great jockey – Angela says he's got real stickability. He helps her

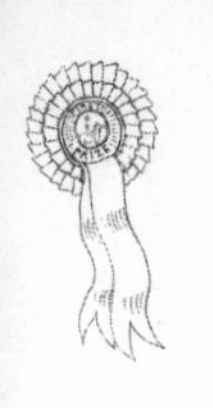

with all the young horses. Cally really fancies him, although she'll tell you that she doesn't!"

Tilly peered inside the barn. Mia stayed back.

Magic Spirit was in the shadows, munching hay. It was good to see he had an appetite back. He saw Tilly and stepped forward. Cautiously, he dipped the tip of his nose outside, as though he was testing the air. Tilly reached up her hand and let him sniff it. She gently told him she was pleased to see him.

"You're so brave," said Mia admiringly.

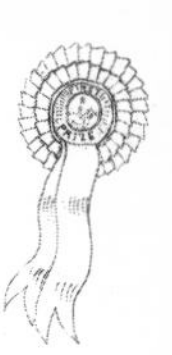

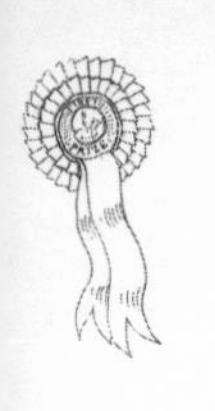

"When I know a horse is likely to get freaked out, it makes me nervous."

"That's the thing," said Tilly, scratching Magic Spirit's neck. "I think he can sense our feelings – if we feel confident around him, he'll feel confident around us."

Eight

Over the next few days, Tilly couldn't wait to visit Silver Shoe Farm again. She swapped phone numbers with Cally and Mia, and on Thursday evening she got a text saying:

ME AND CAL GOING 2 STABLES TOMOZ B4 SCHOOL.
WANNA COME? PICK U UP AT 7. MIA. X

Tilly was too excited to worry about getting up early. She was out of bed before her alarm went off.

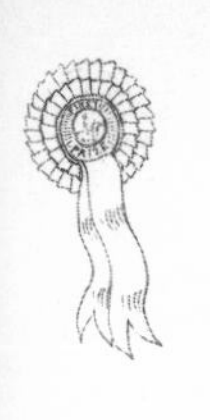

Mia's mum picked her up and drove the three girls to Silver Shoe. She told them they had to be ready to leave by eight-fifteen, in order to get to school on time. She waited for them in the car, checking emails on her Blackberry.

"Right," said Cally bossily, as they walked through the gate. "This morning, Tilly, you can help us muck out – there's a not-so-glamorous side to keeping a pony that I think you need to know about." She smiled.

Tilly didn't mind at all. To her it was all part of the fun of being at the farm – and she knew how important it was for the horses to have food, clean water and fresh bedding. Thankfully she was prepared. She was wearing a pair of jeans and an old sweatshirt. Her uniform was folded neatly in her bag, away from the dust and dirt.

The girls greeted Rosie and led her outside, then they went into the stable.

"We have to do this every day," explained Mia. "We start by clearing out the muck."

She pointed towards a pile of manure, and nudged Cally towards it.

"You always make me do this bit," groaned Cally, attacking the manure with her special shavings fork. "You're such a wimp, Mia!"

Mia giggled.

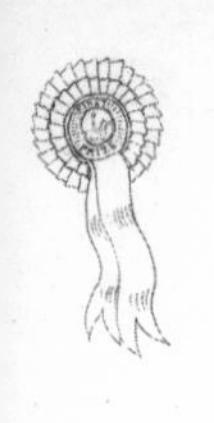

"Next, we dig out any wet bedding and replace it if necessary. Princess Rosie likes her layer of bedding to be comfy and thick, fluffed up like pillows for when she lies down – of course!"

"I can do that," said Tilly helpfully, picking up the fork.

"We're lucky. Shavings are much easier to muck out than straw," said Cally. "Rosie is on shavings because she has an allergy to straw. The odd racehorses Angela has in go on shredded newspaper, which is completely dust free. I'll go and get some fresh water and hay. Just watch out for the mice!"

The idea of mice didn't bother Tilly. She loved all animals.

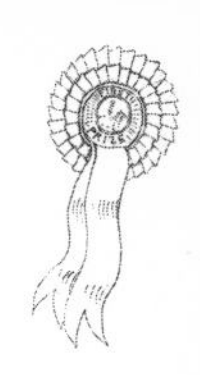

To Tilly's delight, the girls invited her back to Silver Shoe after school. Twice in one day! This time, she visited Magic Spirit. He was looking much healthier and most of his sores had cleared up. But to Tilly, he still seemed sad and lonely which, in turn, made her feel sad. She wondered why he refused to come out of his barn – especially when there were so many lovely horses around the farm for him to make friends with.

Meanwhile, Angela was in the yard, lugging bags of feed down from a lorry. Tilly offered to help.

"Hello you. What's up?" said Angela, immediately noticing Tilly's mood. "It's a wonderful warm evening, and you've got a glum face."

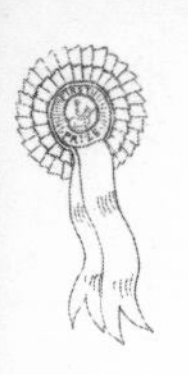

"I wish," said Tilly. "I *wish* that Magic Spirit would come out of his barn. It must be so lonely in there. All the others are going off and having fun, and he's on his own in the dark."

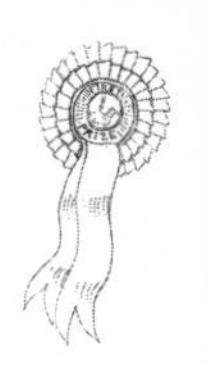

"Mmm, he'll come out when he's ready, I'm sure, but maybe he feels safe in there. You've done a great job earning his trust, Tilly. Don't feel bad."

Tilly nodded.

"My dad," explained Angela, "has trained hundreds of horses. And he says the most important thing of all is not to rush anything."

"Act like you've got ten years with a horse and the job will take ten minutes. Act like you've got ten minutes and it will probably take ten years!" said a voice behind them.

It was Jack Fisher. He'd overheard them talking. "It's an old cowboy saying," he said. "And a true one. That little fella, Magic Spirit, needs lots of patience and love. We don't know anything about what he's been through or what frightens him. It takes time to understand an animal who's been neglected, or through some kind of trauma."

"Maybe he's ready for you to groom him," said Angela to Tilly. "His coat really

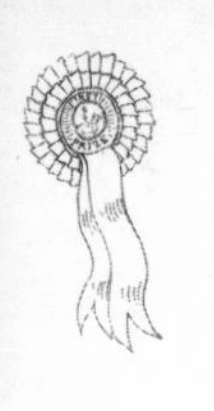

needs some attention and I'm sure he'd like *you* to do it more than anyone else."

"Can I really?" said Tilly.

"I think it would be a good thing for both of you. I'll ask Duncan to give you some help, until Magic Spirit gets used to it all."

Tilly met Duncan in the clubroom, and she remembered what Mia had said about Cally fancying him. He *was* quite good-looking, with messy hair and twinkling blue eyes. He was suntanned from being outside a lot. But too old for Cally, thought Tilly – although maybe he and Angela would make a nice couple.

As they fetched a grooming kit from the tack room, Duncan explained how Angela had kindly given him the job of head boy when he had no money.

"I used to groom horses for the kids at Cavendish Hall – and then Jack Fisher spotted me at a local show. He said I had the makings

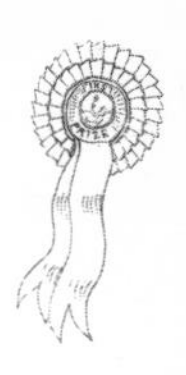

of a top jockey. He introduced me to the lovely Angela, and the rest is history. I'm going to win big for the Fishers one day. You watch."

As soon as Tilly popped her head over Magic's door, he stepped forward and wickered softly. Duncan explained to Tilly that this was a sign of recognition, like mares and their foals make to each other.

Tilly was overjoyed. Quietly, she stepped into his box, taking her time, reassuring Magic that everything was fine. But as soon as Duncan followed her, Magic snorted, and straightaway became restless. So Duncan went back to the door, fascinated by what he saw.

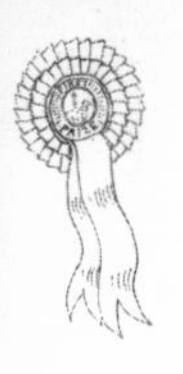

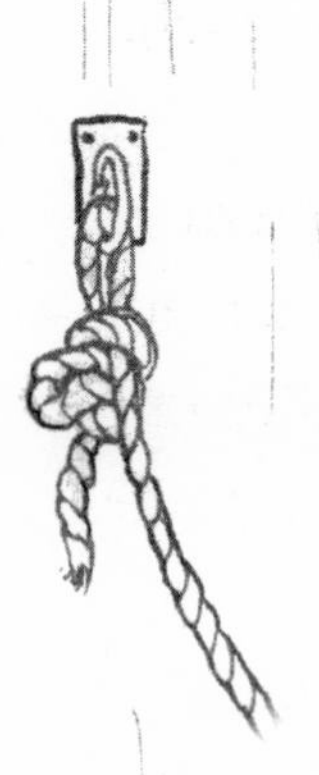

Tilly gently scratched Magic's favourite spot at the base of his neck, by his withers, and as he lowered his head, she gave him a carrot. Very slowly, she was able to put the head collar on him, but she didn't tie him up because she knew he would feel constrained. She just looped the rope through the ring next to his manger.

Starting at the base of his neck, she used the soft body brush on his thin coat. Gradually, much to Duncan's amazement, Magic started to relax, and enjoy this whole new experience of pampering. All the time, Tilly was chatting away to Magic, telling him about her dream of one day becoming a famous show jumper.

"Here," said Duncan, passing her a comb. "See if you can tidy up his mane and tail, but go carefully, because it looks as though there are a few knots in there."

As soon as Tilly tried to touch his mane,

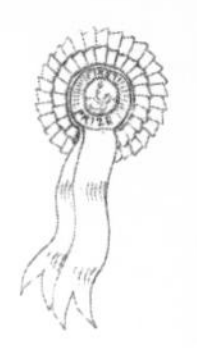

Magic got anxious and immediately tossed his head so that Tilly could no longer reach. She moved onto his tail instead.

Tilly began to work the comb through Magic Spirit's tail, and as she did so, several long hairs came loose. She gathered them up and wound them around her wrist next to her bracelet.

"That's an unusual piece of jewellery," said Duncan, staring at her horsehair bracelet. "And yet, it's strangely familiar. I think I've seen one like it somewhere before . . . can't quite remember. Where did you get it?"

Tilly shrugged, because the truth was, she didn't know. The Redbrows had told her she was wearing the bracelet when they adopted her, looped three times around her wrist because she was so little. Now it was only looped twice, because she had grown.

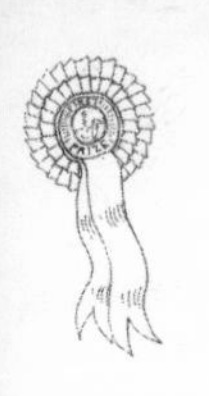

As she finished polishing his coat with a stable rubber, Tilly asked Duncan, "Do you think Magic Spirit will ever want to go outside?"

"Why don't you ask him?" answered Duncan.

So Tilly leaned towards Magic Spirit's ear and asked, and at the same time she pointed towards the open door. Magic Spirit stepped back and began swishing his tail. Tilly knew this meant he was unhappy.

"There's your answer," said Duncan. "Something out there is bothering him – and I think I might know what it is."

Carefully he inspected Magic Spirit's coat, all the time soothing him with his voice.

"Look here," he showed Tilly, lifting Magic Spirit's mane. "Bite marks."

Tilly could see several raised scars, in the shape of teeth.

"Ow . . . that's awful! *Who* would do a thing like that?" she gasped, upset at the thought.

"Not *who*, but *what*. They're not human

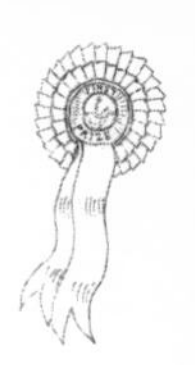

bites. It looks to me like the work of another horse. It happens occasionally, I'm afraid. Some horses just don't get along with each other. When they're out in the field they push each other about. Maybe that explains why his owner abandoned him."

"Poor Magic Spirit," said Tilly sniffing as she stroked his forehead. Magic leaned across and rested his nose on her shoulder affectionately.

"It also explains," said Duncan, scratching his head, "why Magic Spirit is wary of going outside – the other horses might be a bother to him. He's probably frightened of being bitten again."

Tilly sighed.

"Don't worry," said Duncan. "We'll work on it. And at least we've learned a bit more about Magic Spirit's background now – I think we'll have to be extra sensitive when grooming his mane and face."

"It's a good job you noticed the marks," said Tilly.

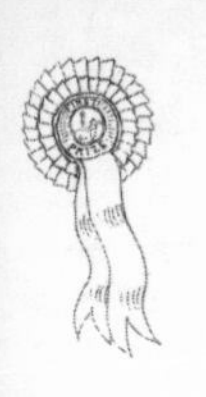

"Well, it's thanks to you that I was able to. Without your help, I wouldn't have been able to get close enough to check. You're the only person who's been able to calm him."

Nine

At last the weekend arrived. Tilly had lost count of how many times she had thought about Magic Spirit and what he was doing. She couldn't wait to see him again. So much had happened. Two weeks ago she was admiring pictures of ponies in magazines. Now she was helping to look after real ones.

On Saturday, Tilly was desperate to go to Silver Shoe Farm, but Mr Redbrow insisted she tidied her bedroom and finished her homework first. This took all morning, and

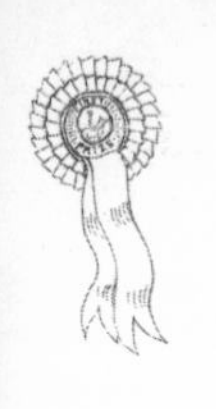

her little brother, Adam, did everything he could to get in the way. While she was hoovering the carpet he kept pulling out the plug. When she was trying to concentrate on her English essay, he turned the television up as loud as he could.

"You little freak!" yelled Tilly. "Go and annoy someone else!"

Adam grinned and chased Scruff into the garden.

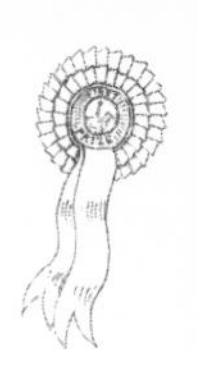

Tilly stared at the pile of schoolbooks in front of her and felt miserable. It was a perfect day for being outside with the horses – brilliant sunshine and blue skies – she could see it through the window, but she was stuck indoors working. A text from Cally only made her feel more frustrated:

R U COMING 2 FARM 2DAY? ME' N' MIA R GOING HACKING. X

She looked at her watch and replied:

MAYBE LATER. HOMEWORK FIRST (GROAN). X

Tilly carried on writing her essay, and as she did, she twiddled with her black horsehair bracelet. She'd put Magic's tail hairs in the special little box she kept on her dressing table. Her thoughts drifted to the idea of him, leaping fences, with her in the saddle. She imagined taking him to an event, maybe even Badminton – going cross-country and winning. She could hear the

commentator's voice: *Tilly Redbrow and Magic Spirit take the lead! Who'd have thought this shy rescue horse would have come as far as he has! What a performance!*

She looked down at her essay and realised she'd written, 'William Shakespeare wrote lots of horses . . .'

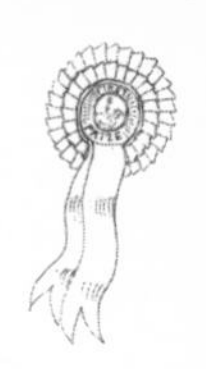

Suddenly her phone buzzed again. It was an answer-phone message from Mia:

"Hi, Tilly, listen, you've got to get to the farm as soon as you can . . .
my battery's about to go . . .
something's happened to Magic Spirit . . .
you need to—"

The line went dead. Tilly felt her heart skip. She tried calling Mia back, but there was no connection. What had happened to Magic Spirit? Had there been an accident? Had he fallen ill?

There was only one way to find out. In a panic, she ran into the garden, where her dad was digging his vegetable patch and her mum was sweeping the path.

"Can I go to the farm? I've got to go to the farm! Can I? *Please!*" she begged, without stopping for breath.

Her parents looked up.

"What's all the fuss about, Tiger Lil'?" said her dad.

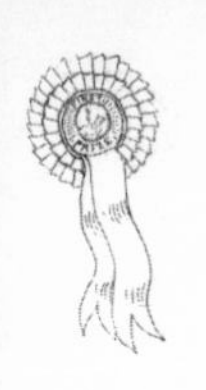

"Magic Spirit! Something's happened – I need to see him!"

"But have you finished your homework?" her dad said, using his sensible teacher's voice.

"Um . . . sort of . . . nearly," said Tilly, flustered.

"I said chores and homework first," he replied, shaking his head. "Come on, it won't take you long. Magic Spirit can wait till you've done that."

"But it might be too *late* by then," cried Tilly. Adam stood behind her pulling faces. "*Please!*" she begged. "Something's happened."

"Maybe," said her mum, seeing how desperate her daughter was. "Maybe I could give you a lift when I drop Adam at football practice – we'll be leaving in ten minutes."

Tilly clapped her hands together and nodded hopefully.

"But what about your homework?" muttered Mr Redbrow, scratching his head.

"She'll finish it tomorrow, won't you, Tilly?"

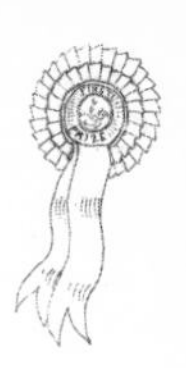

Tilly and her mum winked at each other. Sometimes mums were the best thing in the world.

It took twenty minutes to drop Adam at his football club and then get to Silver Shoe Farm. Tilly fidgeted in her seat, full of nerves, as they drove through the tunnel of trees.

Mrs Redbrow pulled up and Tilly jumped out. She ran up the lane, and through the gate. Without noticing anything that was

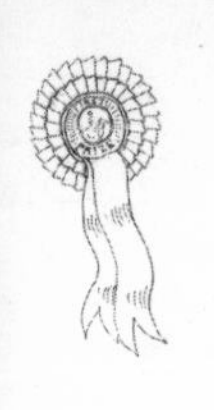

going on in the yard, she went straight to Magic Spirit's barn. He wasn't there!

"Oh no," gasped Tilly. "I'm too late!"

Her eyes started to brim with tears and her hands trembled.

"Hello, Tilly," said a voice behind her. It was Duncan. "Too late for what?"

"Where's Magic Spirit? What's happened?" said Tilly, almost sobbing.

Duncan looked her and smiled.

"You look so worried, Tilly. You'd better come with me," he said, wrapping his arm around her shoulders.

As they walked, Tilly explained:

"I got this answer-phone message from Mia, but she got cut off . . . all it said was that I had to come to the farm, because something has happened to—"

They stopped at a small post and railed paddock behind the stables.

"She's right," nodded Duncan. "Something *has* happened. Look."

And there was Magic Spirit. He was standing outside in the sun, looking relaxed

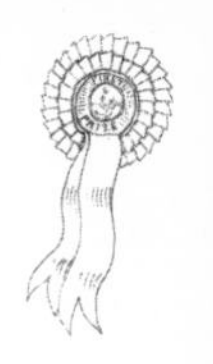

and happy. Next to him was a skewbald miniature pony, only half the size of Magic Spirit!

"What a lovely sight, eh?" said Duncan. "Come and meet Thumbelina – Lina, for short. I borrowed her from a local farmer. I thought she would have a good effect on Magic Spirit, and sure enough, they're getting on brilliantly."

"But I thought . . . oh . . . I was worried something terrible had happened!"

Tilly realised she'd panicked for no reason. Then she saw Mia walking across the stable yard, smiling and waving.

"Hi, Tilly. You got my message then? I was worried it wouldn't reach you. Great news, isn't it?"

Tilly nodded.

"I thought you were trying to tell me something awful had happened!"

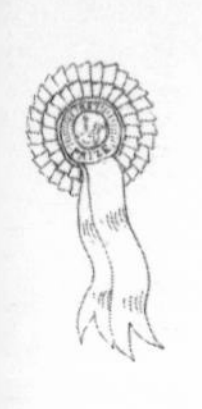

"Sorry," said Mia. "I didn't mean to scare you. I just knew you'd want to see this."

"It's a trick I've used before," explained Duncan, as the girls looked on. "With another rescue horse. Little Lina is so good-natured, and because she's small she isn't a threat. Magic Spirit took to her straightaway. He's made a friend. Hopefully, she'll help him get his confidence back. And who knows? Maybe one day he'll be out grazing with the rest of gang. It's thanks to you, Tilly – you've been so patient with him."

Tilly watched as Magic Spirit sniffed Lina's ears. He seemed happier than ever before. Just then Angela came out of one of the stables. She joined them.

"Excellent," she said. "Duncan always has good ideas about how to settle the horses in. But we

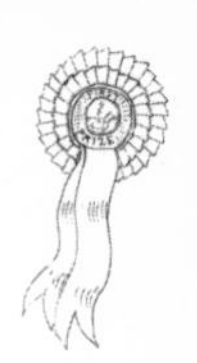

couldn't have done it without you, Tilly – well done. I think Magic Spirit and Lina are going to make a great team."

"Even if they do look a bit mismatched," said Duncan. "Like a comedy double-act!"

Duncan and Angela laughed, but Tilly simply stood back and smiled.

She was so proud of Magic Spirit. For a moment he looked up and met her eye, then carried on grazing. And Tilly knew in her heart that this was going to be the start of great things for him.

Pippa's Top Tips

With good training and positive experiences a horse will develop trust in humans. To build this trust, we need to respond calmly and consistently to their behaviour.

Although horses don't use words, their behaviour can reveal how they feel. Understanding horse behaviour is really important. For example, if a horse swishes its tail or pricks its ears back, it may be afraid. If a horse wickers at you, it's a sign of recognition. Mares make this gentle sound to their foals.

A good way to learn more about horses, whether you own one or not, is to spend time helping out at your local stables or riding school. The Pony Club is also a good starting point. Go to **www.pcuk.org** for more information.

Never be afraid to seek advice from people who have more experience with horses than you.

Owning a horse requires continuous care and commitment. Make sure you can give enough time before you consider this option. You may be able to share the responsibilities with a friend.

Always be aware of the horse's hind legs. Even the quietest horse will kick out at a fly, and if you're in the wrong place at the wrong time, you'll get hurt.

Always check your horse's legs for cuts or swellings before you get on to ride. If you don't, you could cause more damage, or even lameness.

A set of horse shoes normally last around five to six weeks. Most good stables will keep a notebook listing all the dates of when the horses were last shod.

Make sure your horse is safely tied, but use a quick-release, or slip-knot. Some horses don't like the idea of being constrained and it makes them panic.

There are lots of different brushes for grooming horses: a Dandy brush is stiff-bristled, used to loosen dirt – work it in circular motions across the body, but be gentle around the thinner-skinned areas; a stable rubber is a soft rag used to remove any remaining dirt – it makes the horse's coat lovely and shiny; finally, use a comb and conditioning spray to work through the mane and tail.

Acknowledgements

Three years ago when my autobiography was published I never imagined that I would find myself writing children's books. Huge thanks go to Louisa Leaman for helping me to bring Tilly to life, and to Jennifer Miles for her wonderful illustrations.

Many thanks to Fiona Kennedy for persuading and encouraging me to search my imagination and for all her hard work, along with the rest of the team at Orion. Due to my riding commitments I am not the easiest person to get hold of as my agent Jonathan Marks at MTC has found. It's a relief he has been able to work on all the agreements for me.

Much of my thinking about Tilly has been done out loud in front of family, friends and godchildren – thank you all for listening.

More than anything I have to acknowledge my four-legged friends – my horses. It is thanks to them, and the great moments I have had with them, that I was able to create a girl, Tilly, who like me follows her passions.

Pippa Funnell
Forest Green, February 2009